NICKELODEON

SpongeBob SquarePants™

Best Bikini Bottom Stories Ever!

Simon Spotlight/Nickelodeon
New York   London   Toronto   Sydney

Based on the TV series *SpongeBob SquarePants*™
created by Stephen Hillenburg as seen on Nickelodeon™

SIMON SPOTLIGHT
An imprint of Simon & Schuster Children's Publishing Division
1230 Avenue of the Americas, New York, New York 10020
Manufactured in the United States of America   1010 LAK
10 9 8 7 6 5 4
ISBN 978-1-4169-9931-7
These titles were originally published individually by Simon Spotlight.

This book belongs to

_____

TABLE OF CONTENTS

by Kelli Chipponeri
illustrated by Dave Aikins

The Bikini Bottom Relay Race
was just three days away. It only
happened once every five years!
SpongeBob and his friends
could not wait to compete.

It was the first day of practice.
SpongeBob, Patrick, Sandy, Gary,
Mr. Krabs, and Squidward were each
going to compete in an event.
"Team," said Squidward. "We have to
train hard if we are going to win
the golden booty treasure chest.
So I am going to coach you!"

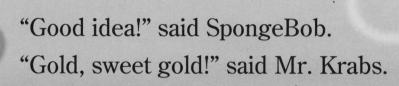

"Good idea!" said SpongeBob.
"Gold, sweet gold!" said Mr. Krabs.

SpongeBob practiced
ship-mast pole vaulting.
He ran, stuck the mast in the sand,
and swung himself over the ship.
"Great job, buddy!" said Sandy.
But Squidward was not impressed.

Then Patrick practiced
the sailing long jump.
He ran, flaring out his arms
and legs to jump far.
"Jump farther!" called Squidward.

Sandy and Mr. Krabs practiced their
events. Mr. Krabs spun around,
then tossed the sand dollar discus.
Sandy ran and threw the javelin.
"Not good enough!" cried Squidward.
"What is it with you people!?"

Even Gary was going to compete!
He practiced hurdling coral.
"We are never going to win if
you move this slowly, Gary!"
cried Squidward, annoyed.

Then it was Squidward's turn.
He picked up a kelp log
and practiced tossing it.
"Nice throw, Squidward!"
his teammates cheered.

"Team meeting!" called Squidward.
The team jogged over happily.
"Great practice!" cheered Sandy.
"Am I sweaty?" SpongeBob asked.
"Let's do it again!" cried Patrick.
"Meow!" agreed Gary.

"Quiet!" said their coach.
"We will never win first place
   if we compete like that.
   Tomorrow we need to work harder!"
"Okay," said the team, unsure why.

They thought practice went well.
"We have to go for the gold!"
Squidward reminded them.
"Ah, sweet gold!" said Mr. Krabs.

The next day at practice
SpongeBob tried hard to vault high.
"HIGHER!" demanded Squidward.
"We must win that pirate's booty!"

Patrick strained to make his arms
and legs as long as possible.
"LONGER!" Squidward shouted.
"Think about the treasure chest!"

"Spin, Krabs!" cried Squidward.

"Throw it FARTHER, Sandy!"
barked Squidward. "Go for the gold!"

"Faster, Gary! FASTER!"

But Gary still moved too slowly.

"Who am I kidding? We can't win.
I might as well just go home and
hang my head in shame,"
said Squidward, kicking the grass.

TWEET! Squidward blew his whistle.
"Okay people. My mother always says
if I want something done right,
I have to do it myself," he said.

"If I compete in all of the events, we are sure to win! So, tomorrow I am going to practice them all!" Then he stormed off the field.

"Squidward wants to win so badly that he is making us miserable," Sandy told the rest of the gang.

"Yeah. What's the point of being in the relay race if we do not have fun doing it?" asked SpongeBob.

The next day Squidward practiced
all of his teammates' events.

When it was time for his event, Squidward was so tired he could barely throw the log.

"Squidward," Sandy said. "You can't compete in everything. You should trust that we will do our best."

"What if we do not win?" he asked.

"What, no gold?" cried Mr. Krabs.

"Winning isn't everything," Sandy said.
"Stop worrying about winning and enjoy
being teammates with us!"
"Yeah!" agreed the group.
"Not compete just to win?" he said.
"Mmm, I guess we could try it."

The day of the race the team was
warming up, when *TWEET! TWEET!*
"Team meeting!" called Squidward.
The team huddled. "Just do
your best!" Squidward said.
"Go team!" they cheered.

"Fly, SpongeBob, fly!"
cheered Squidward.
"Jump, Patrick, jump!
"Throw, Sandy, throw!"
coached Squidward.
"Spin, Krabs baby, spin!"

"Hurdle, Gary, hurdle!"
cheered Squidward, as Gary
trailed behind the other hurdlers.

Squidward picked up the
kelp log and let it go.
The log flew through the air.
"Go, Squidward!" cheered his team.

"Second place," sighed Squidward.
"True, we didn't win the gold,"
said SpongeBob. "But we worked well
together and had fun! We could have
come in third."

"Of course," replied Squidward,
"if you weren't such slugs,
we could have won, but . . ."
"SLUGS!" the team cried.
Squidward smiled. "I mean slugs
in the kindest way."

Squidward's teammates were right.
They did have a good time. And that
made them all feel like winners!

My Trip to Atlantis
by SpongeBob SquarePants

adapted by Sarah Willson
based on the teleplay "Atlantis SquarePantis"
by Dani Michaeli and Steven Banks
illustrated by The Artifact Group

It all began when I was blowing
bubbles with Patrick.
"Watch this, Patrick," I said.
I blew and blew. My bubble was huge!
But then it closed in around us and
began to float away—with us inside!

"Aaaah! What have I done?" I cried.
We floated for a long time.
We finally ended up in a cave.
That's when we heard a *pop*!
The bubble popped on something sharp!

"What is that? It looks like
an old coin," I said.
It looked ancient,
so we decided to take it to
the Bikini Bottom Museum.

We met Sandy and Squidward there.
"Where did you get that?"
Squidward asked.
"This old coin?" I said.
"That's the missing half of the
Atlantian amulet!" said Squidward.

We had no idea what he meant.
"Missing omelet?" asked Patrick.
"No, *amulet*! It is from the lost
city of Atlantis!" Squidward said.
Then he showed us a mural
of Atlantis on the wall.

"They say the streets of Atlantis
  are paved in gold," said Squidward.
"What?" yelled Mr. Krabs.
  He had just appeared out of nowhere!

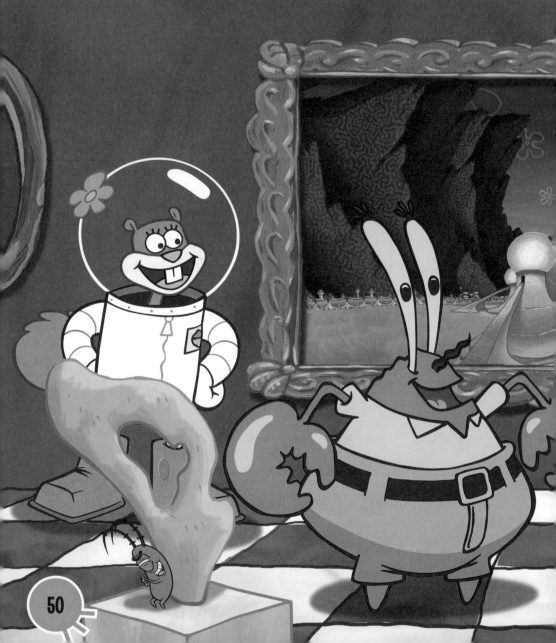

Squidward told us that Atlantis was
known for its arts and sciences.
"They invented weapons, too.
But the people of Atlantis were
peaceful and never used them,"
he said.

"What's that bubble doing there?"
I asked Squidward.
"That's the world's oldest bubble.
The real bubble is in Atlantis."

Then Sandy had an idea.

"Connect the two halves!" she said.

"They might take us to Atlantis!"

So Squidward put them together.

There was a loud *boom*!

Then we saw bright beams of light.

All of a sudden a van appeared!
The amulet floated over to it
and clicked into place.
"All aboard!" said Sandy.
Zoom! We were flying!
We flew and flew until—*crash*!
We were finally there!

We saw a great big palace.

"Welcome to Atlantis!" a man said.

"I am King Lord Royal Highness."

"I am SpongeBob," I said.

"These are my friends."

"Would you care for a tour
  of our great city?" he asked.

We all said yes, and off we went!

"For centuries we have been experts
in art, science, weapons, and
treasure collecting," said the king.
Mr. Krabs jumped up and down.
"I love treasures!" he said.

So the king took us to the
treasure room.
"Help yourself!" he told Mr. Krabs.
We left Mr. Krabs there.
Patrick and I just wanted to see
the world's oldest bubble.

Then Sandy asked to see
the Hall of Inventions.
The Atlantians had invented a lot!
They even had a machine that turned
everything into ice cream!
We left Sandy there to explore.
We kept looking for the bubble.

Squidward wanted to see the art.
We left him in the Hall of Arts.
Finally, I blurted out,
"Please, oh please, may we see
the ancient bubble?"
The king smiled. "Of course!"

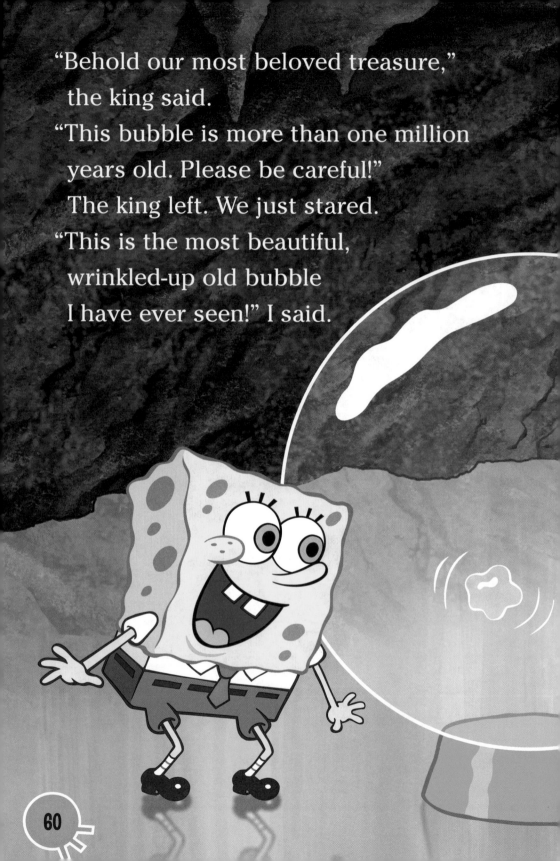

"Behold our most beloved treasure,"
the king said.
"This bubble is more than one million
years old. Please be careful!"
The king left. We just stared.
"This is the most beautiful,
wrinkled-up old bubble
I have ever seen!" I said.

Patrick thought so too.
He decided to take a picture
of us with the bubble.

Click! Pop!

"Pat, did you hear something?"

Patrick and I looked at each other.

"Oh, no!" we both yelled.

"We destroyed the most ancient,
priceless treasure in Atlantis!
How will we tell the king?" I asked.

That evening at our dinner feast
we told the king about the bubble.
He just laughed.
"That's not the real bubble.
This is!" he said, showing it off.
But then Patrick took a picture of
the real bubble.
And this one popped too!

"We are so sorry!" I cried out.
The king's face just darkened.
"Guards!" he yelled.
"Do not let them get away!"
"RUN!" shouted Sandy.
We ran and ran.
The guards chased after us.

We ran straight into Plankton.
He was driving a huge tank.
"Cower before me!" he said
with an evil laugh. "Now I have
the most powerful weapon!
Prepare to taste my wrath!"

He pressed the button.

I was so afraid!

Splat!

"Plankton's wrath tastes like
ice cream!" said Patrick.
"Mmm!" I said, shoveling it into my mouth.

"This thing blasts ICE CREAM?"
said Plankton angrily.
He climbed down and began
to kick the tank.
"OW!" he yelled.

We were happy that we were saved from Plankton, but we knew the king was still angry with us.

But then the king smiled.
"Look! A talking speck!" he said.
"It will make a great replacement
for our ruined national treasure."
"I will get you!" yelled Plankton
as the king picked him up.
"Yes, this is much better than our
dusty old bubble," he said.

We got back in the van.

We waved good-bye to the king.

He seemed so happy that we had come!

And that whole bubble thing
worked out in the end too.
Boy, Atlantis sure is a great place!

We waved good-bye to Plankton.
I hope he has as much fun in Atlantis
as we did!

MY NAME IS CHEESEHEAD

adapted by Erica David
based on the teleplay "Who Bob What Pants?"
by Casey Alexander, Zeus Cervas, and Steven Banks
illustrated by Victoria Miller

One day I woke up and found myself
in a strange place.
Where am I? I wondered.
Uh . . . **who** am I?

I had no idea how I got here.
Two friendly people helped me out.
They told me my name was
CheeseHead BrownPants.
CheeseHead BrownPants?
That didn't sound right.

I checked my pockets for clues
to help me remember.
All I found was a bubble wand
and some bubble soap.
Suddenly my new friends screamed
and ran away.

I started walking to look for
some answers.
Soon I arrived in New Kelp City.
The streets were dark and empty.

I bumped into someone by mistake.

"Sorry, sir," I said.

"You are not sorry!" the man cried.

"You were trying to take money
from my pocket!"

"I would never!" I said.

"Yeah, right! If you are looking
for money, get a job!" he said.

I went to look for a job at the bank.
"Mr. BrownPants, you did not
   fill out this form," said the bank lady.
"I know. I can't seem to remember
   anything," I said.
"Do you have any special skills?"
   she asked.

"I can do this!" I said, taking out
my wand. I blew a shiny, soapy bubble.
The lady gasped and told me
to leave!

Luckily I found a job at a construction site.

"Thanks for the job," I told my boss.

"BrownPants, that hammer is not moving fast enough!" he shouted.

"Yes, sir!" I replied.

I blew a large bubble and rode it up the building, hammering faster than before.
When my boss saw the bubble, he yelled, "BrownPants, you can't do that here! You're fired!"

I wandered around New Kelp City,
feeling very sad and lonely.
I didn't understand why everyone
was acting so strangely.
At last I met some people standing
by a fire.

"Hey, do you mind if I blow bubbles?"
I asked. "It will cheer me up."
"You can't do that here!" they said.
"Don't worry," I said, as I took
a deep breath and blew a shiny,
soapy bubble.

Suddenly a street gang appeared.
"Do you have any idea who we are?"
the leader asked.
I shook my head.
"We are the Bubble-Poppin' Boys,"
he said. "Nobody blows bubbles
on our turf!"

"Yeah, **nobody**," his friend said.
"We have ways of dealing with
bubble blowers like you,"
the leader added.

I started to run as fast as I could.
But the Bubble-Poppin' Boys
chased after me!
I had to think of a way to escape.

Suddenly I had an idea.
I blew some bubbles and
climbed them just like stairs.
This made the gang more angry.

Then I blew bubbles shaped
like a raft and an oar.
I paddled away from the
Bubble-Poppin' Boys.
But this time they were ready.
The gang took out slingshots.
They launched pebbles into the air—
and popped my bubble raft!
What was I going to do now?

I took a deep breath and blew
one giant bubble that closed around
the Bubble-Poppin' Boys.
They were trapped!
The bubble floated away
with the Boys inside.

Suddenly everyone ran out
into the street and started to cheer,
"You have freed the city!
Now we can blow bubbles again!"
They were so happy that
they made me the mayor
of New Kelp City!

Later I spoke to the crowd.
"Citizens of New Kelp City," I said,
"I promise you that it will always
be safe to blow bubbles in the streets,
or my name isn't CheeseHead
BrownPants!"

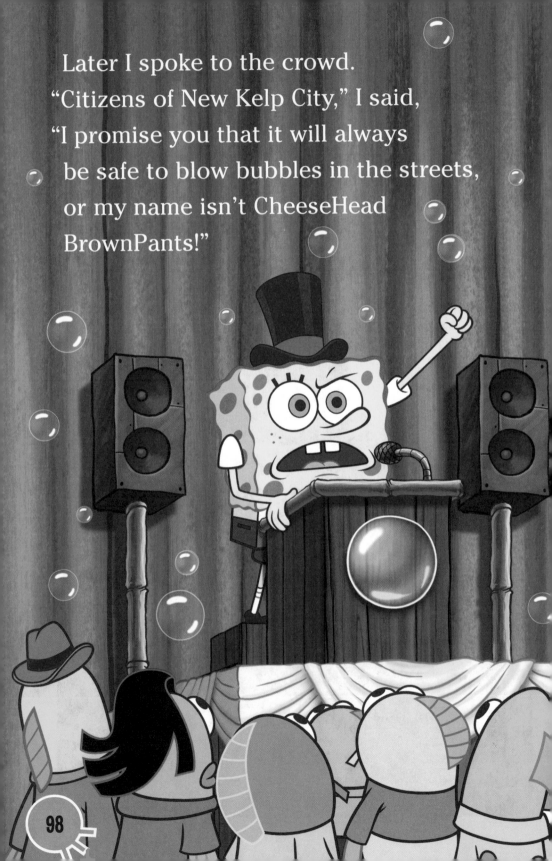

"But your name isn't CheeseHead
   BrownPants. It's SpongeBob
   SquarePants," said a squirrel
   I had never seen before.
"Who are you?" I asked.
   She said her name was Sandy.

"I am your best friend, Patrick,"
said a big pink sea star.
I shook my head.
"SpongeBob, come back with us
to Bikini Bottom," said Sandy.
"It will help you remember."

"I can't. I have an important job
to do as mayor," I said. "In fact
I have a meeting right now."
A boat arrived to take me
to my meeting. But it took me to
Bikini Bottom instead!

"Here it is: the Krusty Krab,"
said Sandy. "You must remember
this place."
"Nope," I replied.

A crab stepped forward.

"SpongeBob, stop kidding and start
frying up those Patties!" he said.

"I was a fry cook before?" I asked.

"The best," said the crab.

"I am sure being a fry cook
is great," I said, "but I prefer
being mayor of a major city."

I began to walk toward the door
when suddenly—*bonk*—
something hit me on the head!
"Ouch!" I cried.
I rubbed my head and looked around.

At that moment my memory came back.
"Hey, I remember this place!" I said.
"SpongeBob's back!" Sandy cheered.
"Hooray!" cried Patrick.
"Into the kitchen SpongeBob,
   me boy," said Mr. Krabs.

"I am sorry, Mr. Krabs, but the people of New Kelp City need me," I said.
Just then there was a report on TV.
"This just in: New Kelp City is in trouble!" the reporter said.

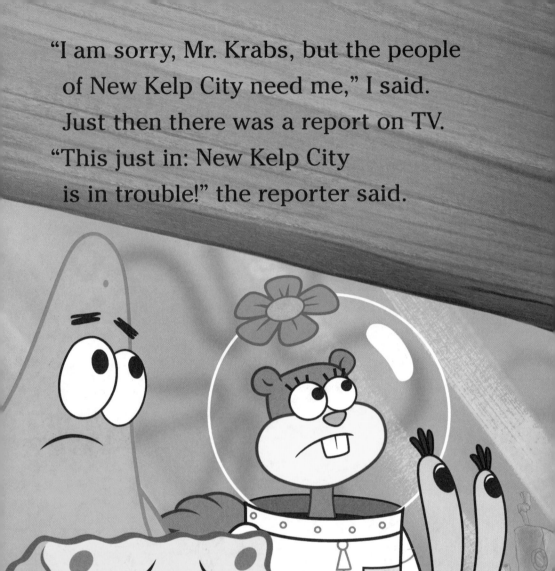

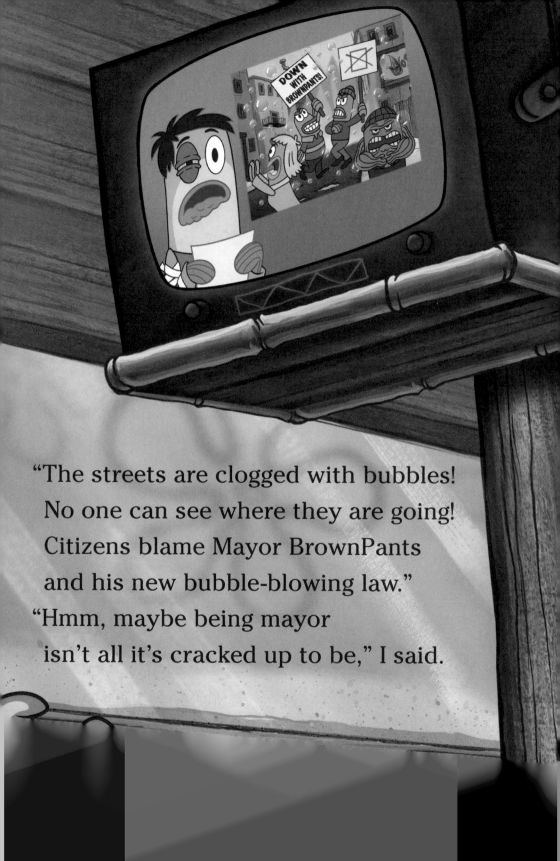

"The streets are clogged with bubbles!
No one can see where they are going!
Citizens blame Mayor BrownPants
and his new bubble-blowing law."
"Hmm, maybe being mayor
isn't all it's cracked up to be," I said.

"This is the life!"

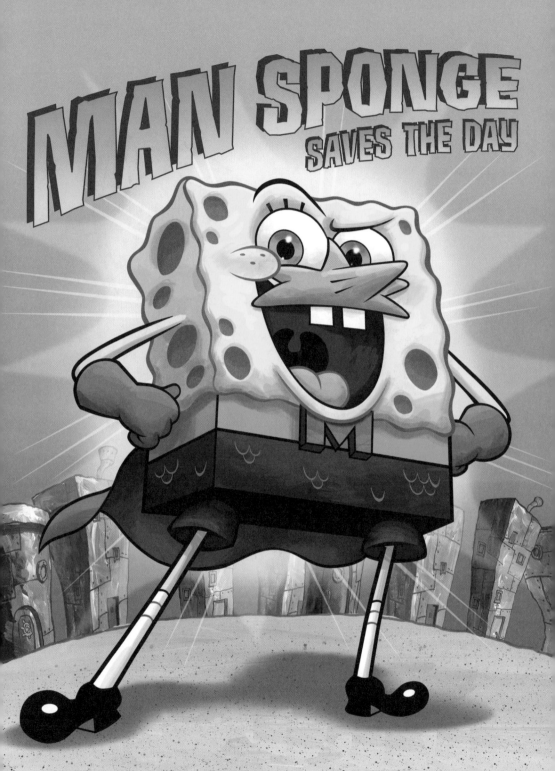

by Sarah Willson
illustrated by The Artifact Group

"Have a great trip!" said SpongeBob.
"I will water your plants
  while you are away!"
"Thanks," said Mermaidman.

"Feel free to borrow
the invisible bicycle—
if you can find it,"
added Barnacleboy.

I will take care of everything,
said SpongeBob.
"After all, you will only be gone
for two weeks.
What could go wrong?"

Meanwhile, in Plankton's lair . . .

Stinky Squ
Dirty Bubbl
Slimy Pete
Terrible Tuna
Bad Blowfish
Ugly Urchin
Ghastly Grouper
Sinister Squid
Man Ray

"Aha! They are leaving town!"
said Plankton as he cackled.
"I will invite all the bad guys
to Bikini Bottom!"
He got on the phone and hit
every number on his speed dial.

The bad guys arrived quickly.
"Welcome, fellow do-no-gooders!"
said Plankton. "Mermaidman and
Barnacleboy are out of town.
Now we can take over the world!"
All the bad guys nodded and
laughed.

"And with those two out of the way,
I can finally get my hands on
that Krabby Patty formula!"
Plankton added to himself.

I think I will go for a bike ride,
said SpongeBob.
He looked around for
the invisible bicycle.

Three hours later, SpongeBob
found the bicycle.
He opened the garage door
and yelled, "Oh, no!"

Bikini Bottom was in big trouble!
"Help!" everyone cried.
"Where are Mermaidman
   and Barnacleboy?"

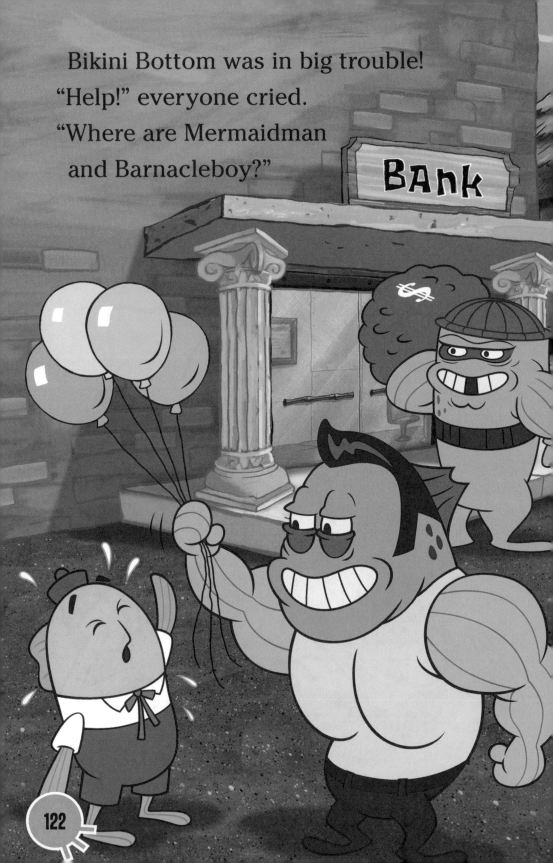

Everyone was so scared,
they were leaving Bikini Bottom.
Even the police were running away!
SpongeBob knew that it was
up to him to save the day.
"This," he said, "is a job for . . ."

NOW
LEAVING
BIKINI
BOTTOM

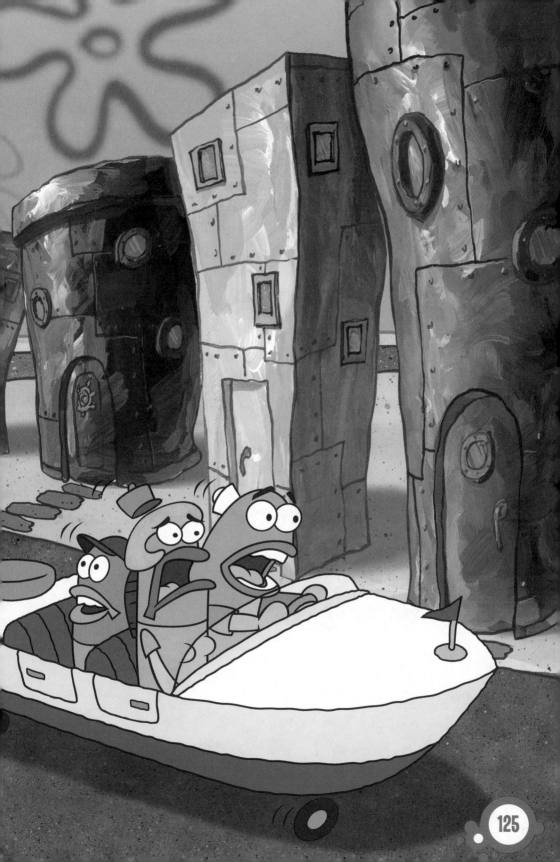

"Man Sponge!"

"Off I go to defend the weak, protect the helpless, and fight evil!" said Man Sponge. "To the invisible bicycle!"

"Wait. Where did I park it?" And one hour later, off he went.

"Stop, thief!" shouted Man Sponge.

But the thief did not stop.

"Well, that didn't work,"

Man Sponge said. "What do I do now?"

Just then the thief tripped over
the invisible bicycle.
The bag of money flew into
Man Sponge's hands.
"I did it!" he cried happily.
"Help!" someone else shouted.

Some bad guys had tied up
the ice-cream guy—and Patrick!
The bad guys were pushing all the
ice-cream tubs out of the truck!

Man Sponge crept up to the truck
and took the bad guys' rope.
Twirling it like a lasso, he caught
the two guys and tied them up.
Then he untied Patrick and the
ice-cream man.

Man Sponge saw someone ring
a doorbell, then run away.
He saw Man Ray pop bubble wrap
in the library!
He saw someone else paint on a sign.
"Freeze!" yelled Man Sponge.
But no one froze.

All these bad guys were heading
toward Man Sponge.
So he squirted bubble-blowing liquid
on the ground.

"Whoa!" yelled the bad guys.
They slipped and slid
on the bubble stuff—
right into Man Sponge's
huge jellyfishing net!

Suddenly Man Sponge heard "Help!"
It was Mr. Krabs.
"Somebody has stolen the secret
Krabby Patty formula!"
he yelled.

"It must be Plankton!" said Man Sponge.
He sprang into action.

"Stop, Plankton!" yelled Man Sponge.
But Plankton did not stop.
Man Sponge pulled something
out of his costume.
TWANG! His tightie-whities
knocked Plankton down.

Man Sponge trapped Plankton.
"That should hold you
    until the police return," he said.
"I will get you next time, Man Sponge,"
    said Plankton.

At last, all was well
in Bikini Bottom.
Everyone came back.
So did the police.
They put the bad guys behind bars.

"Thank you, Man Sponge!"
everyone shouted.

"Aw, it was nothing,"
said Man Sponge.